Lost in Space
An Up2U Action Adventure

by Jan Fields

illustrated by Oriol Vidal

Calico

An Imprint of Magic Wagon
abdopublishing.com

For Collin, who knows how to make every day an adventure. -JF

To my family, the best ones. -OV

abdopublishing.com

Published by Magic Wagon, a division of ABDO, PO Box 398166, Minneapolis, Minnesota 55439. Copyright © 2018 by Abdo Consulting Group, Inc. International copyrights reserved in all countries. No part of this book may be reproduced in any form without written permission from the publisher. Calico™ is a trademark and logo of Magic Wagon.

Printed in the United States of America, North Mankato, Minnesota.
052017
092017

 **THIS BOOK CONTAINS RECYCLED MATERIALS**

Written by Jan Fields
Illustrated by Oriol Vidal
Edited by Bridget O'Brien
Design Contributors: Christina Doffing and Laura Mitchell

Publisher's Cataloging-in-Publication Data

Names: Fields, Jan, author. | Vidal, Oriol, illustrator.
Title: Lost in space: an Up2U action adventure / by Jan Fields ; illustrated by Oriol Vidal.
Other titles: An Up2U action adventure
Description: Minneapolis, MN : Magic Wagon, 2018. | Series: Up2U adventures
Summary: Nick is the only kid on the first planet-based space colony, so when he receives a robot for his birthday, the duo sets out to explore the outside world, but they get lost along the way and it's up to the reader to help them find their way.
Identifiers: LCCN 2017930886 | ISBN 9781532130304 (lib. bdg.) | ISBN 9781614798675 (ebook) | ISBN 9781614798729 (Read-to-me ebook)
Subjects: LCSH: Plot-your-own stories. | Birthdays--Juvenile fiction. | Robots--Juvenile fiction.
Classification: DDC [Fic]--dc23
LC record available at http://lccn.loc.gov/2017930886

TABLE OF CONTENTS

Chapter
→ 1 ←

Happy Birthday, I Think

Nick began drawing a venus flytrap next to a pitcher plant and a sundew on his computer table. He imagined the plant's special leaves snapping shut to catch bugs. He knew he'd never really see any of the cool, different Earth plants that ate bugs.

The colony gardeners mainly grew beans and lettuce. They also grew a few other things to eat. Of course, even if the gardeners would let Nick grow venus flytraps or any of the other bug-eating plants, he wouldn't have any flies to feed them.

Nick spun in his chair. He looked out the one round window in his room. His mom once told him there were always bugs buzzing around you when you went outside on Earth.

Nick didn't get outside much here on Colony Alpha. But when he did, he'd never seen any bugs.

Through the window, he saw blue-green moss carpeting the ground around the colony and the shadowy edge of the fluff tree woods. Moss and fluff trees were boring. Nick was pretty sure the first Earth colony was on the most boring planet in the universe.

Nick sighed. He wouldn't be so bored if his mom were home. She'd be making a birthday cake and telling him Earth stories. She'd have some great present hidden.

But his mom was overdue from a mission with five other scientists. No one knew where they were.

Nick pressed his nose against the window. *I miss you, Mom.*

Before they left, Nick begged to go along. If they had let him go, he might have found some cool plants and animals. And he would know exactly where his mom was. He never got to go on any of the missions. He barely got to go outside.

Nick's dad said it wasn't safe outside of the colony. He said Nick was special. But Nick didn't feel special. As the only kid on Colony Alpha, he was miserable, lonely, and bored.

There was a sharp knock on the door. Nick spun around in his chair. His dad stuck his head through the doorway. He looked tired. He had looked tired ever since Mom left on the mission. Now he hardly ever came back to their quarters.

Dad's hair stuck up in spots from running his fingers through it. Mom called it Dad's puff. Nick could hear her saying, "You can always tell how hard your dad is working by the size of his puff."

Dad tapped Nick on the head. "Happy Birthday! I bet you thought I forgot! Come with me to the lab. I have a present for you."

Nick hopped up and followed his dad out of their quarters. He really was surprised his dad remembered his birthday.

It was always his mom who planned birthdays. She found fun things for Nick to do, while Dad disappeared into the lab. This year, Nick hadn't thought anyone would celebrate his birthday.

With the shushing sound of an air lock seal, the lab door opened. Nick's dad pointed to a robot standing in the middle of the room.

"This is the project I've been working on for the past month. The first one is just for you." He tapped the robot on a shiny shoulder. "Say hello to Nick."

Lights winked on in the robot's face. It turned to look at Nick with bulging camera eyes. "Hello, Nick."

"A robot," Nick mumbled. "Thanks, Dad."

The colony was full of robots already. Some were small and scrambled around on multiple spikey legs. Some were bigger than a person and rolled along on thick treads. Some never moved, staying rooted in one spot to do their job. They had robots to collect samples and robots to build things. They had robots to grow food. They even had robot doctors.

Why would his dad think Nick needed another robot around? "What am I supposed to do with it?" Nick asked.

The robot spoke in a flat voice. "We can play games and have lots of fun together, Nick. I have a full encyclopedia of jokes and riddles, Nick. Why did the feathered farm creature cross the road, Nick?"

"Feathered farm creature?" Nick said, looking at his dad.

"A chicken."

Nick turned back to the robot. "I don't know. I've never seen a real chicken. Or a road."

"Input accepted. Updating joke file." The robot whirred softly for a moment. "Why did the colonist cross the corridor, Nick?"

"I still don't know."

"To get to the other side, Nick." The robot's whirring grew louder and it made an odd wheezing noise. *Was it supposed to be laughing?*

Nick rolled his eyes and turned to his dad. "Can you make him stop doing that?"

His dad looked confused. "Doing what? Telling jokes?"

"Well, yes, that too. But can you make him quit saying my name at the end of every sentence? It's creepy."

"I can stop saying your name at the end of every sentence," the robot offered in its flat voice. "But I really like telling jokes. I like to have fun, Nick."

At that, his dad clapped his hands. "See? You two will have a great time."

Nick looked at his dad's happy grin. Then he looked to the robot's fixed stare. An icy chill slipped down his back. *Why do I have the feeling this is the worst present ever?*

Chapter
→ 2 ←

Forbidden Field Trip

Nick saw his dad's smile fade. He really was trying. "I'm sure I can do lots of stuff with a robot like this," Nick said, trying to sound excited.

His dad smiled again. "You can. This is a totally new design in biomechanical original building. I wanted to make a robot who could think for itself. If robots can think, they can deal with changing situations and unexpected problems. Then they can be sent alone on missions. This is the first robot from my new design."

Nick felt a rush of anger. If his dad had made the robot sooner, it could have gone on the mission. Then his mom could have stayed in the colony where she was safe. But he knew there was no point saying that to his dad. "That's really interesting," he said instead.

"The robot will learn problem solving and decision-making from you. You'll be its teacher," his dad said. "Plus, it is connected to the colony data cloud. It can help you with your homework. That means it'll be like a teacher for you too."

"Sounds great," Nick said. A teacher is the perfect birthday present to go with his rotten life.

His dad shook his finger. "Keep in mind, it won't do your homework for you. No cheating."

"I don't cheat, Dad," Nick said.

"No." His dad laughed nervously. "Of course you don't. That was a joke. A bad joke, but a joke."

Fits right in with the robot's jokes. Nick peered up at the robot's face. "So what do I call it?"

"Whatever you want. Why don't you guys play catch in the gym? It would be good for you to get more exercise, Nick." His dad flapped his hands at them. "You don't want to start looking like your old dad."

Nick rolled his eyes as he trudged to the door. The gym was turned into a hydro-garden months ago. His mom would have known that. "Sure, Dad," he said. "Come on, Bob."

"Bob?" the robot echoed as it clumped after him. "Is that my designation, Nick?"

"I meant it more as a nickname. Dad said you're a biomechanical original build, so I'll call you Bob. If that's okay with you."

The robot turned its blank stare to Nick. "Bob is an excellent choice. According to the colony files, no other robot has a nickname. Only people. I like having a nickname. Thank you, Nick."

When they reached the hall, Nick put his hands on his hips. "So what do I do with you?"

"We could play catch, Nick," Bob said.

"I thought you were going to stop that."

The robot whirred softly. "Stop what, Nick?"

"Stop saying my name after every sentence."

"I did stop. I instituted a new pattern where I only say your name at the end of each block of conversation. The blocks may contain several sentences, Nick."

"It still sounds creepy. How about you cut back to only saying my name when you need to get my attention for something, okay?"

"That is acceptable. Do you want to go play catch now?"

"We can't. The gym is gone."

"I am aware of all changes in the colony map. We cannot play catch in the gym," the robot said. "We can play catch outside. It will offer more space for physical activity. And it will allow me to interact with unplanned situations. That will be helpful to my programming."

"I'm not allowed outside alone," Nick said.

"You would not be alone. I will be with you."

"I'm not sure."

The robot's insides whirred. "Maybe you would like to hear another riddle. Why did the colonist throw a digital timekeeping device out the colony doors?"

"I don't know."

"He wanted to see time fly," Bob wheezed.

Nick couldn't imagine listening to Bob's jokes all day. "Enough jokes. Let's go outside."

The robot easily opened the code-locked outer colony doors. Nick peeked out at the clearing and

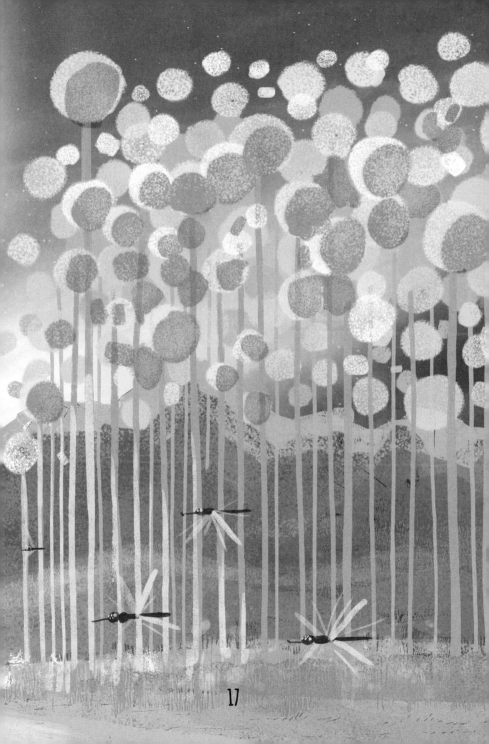

17

fuzzy, blue-green moss. His mom had gone out that door and never come back.

Nick stared across the clearing and wished his mom would appear. She would step from between the tall, skinny trees and wave.

Bob reached out and gave Nick a push. "Come on. Unless you are a feathered farm creature."

"I'm no chicken," Nick snapped. Then he stepped through the door into the forbidden world beyond.

CHAPTER
→ 3 ←

Catch or Caught?

The thick moss in the clearing was softer than the floors in the colony. Nick felt like he was walking on soft springs. He wondered if he could jump higher outside. Maybe he would have the robot measure it sometime.

If his mom came home soon, maybe she could help. She always helped Nick find answers. He looked at the robot's blank face. Bob stopped in the middle of the clearing. Getting answers from the robot would not be the same.

"This will be a good place to play catch, Nick." A small compartment slid open in Bob's chest.

The robot reached in to pull out a ball. Nick laughed as Bob threw a smooth pitch. The ball smacked into Nick's hands. Having a robot might be fun after all.

They tossed the ball back and forth. But Nick kept an eye on the colony doors. Even though coming outside was Bob's idea, Nick knew which one of them would get yelled at by his dad. Nick's mom liked exploring, but his dad liked safety.

Now and then, the doors slid open and one of the colony robots rolled out. The robots didn't pay any attention to Bob or Nick. They rolled through the clearing and into the trees. When the robots passed, Bob stopped playing and watched them.

At one point, Bob stepped in front of one of the robots. "Hello! My nickname is Bob."

The robot simply changed direction and rolled around Bob.

Bob turned its blank face toward Nick. "These other robots are different from me."

"That's for sure," Nick agreed.

"I would like to follow one and see how it carries out its mission."

Nick shrugged. "Sure, that might be fun." He really thought it sounded boring. The colony robots never did anything interesting. But Bob had played catch with him. They could do something Bob liked now.

They followed a small, four-legged robot. The scientists often used them to gather samples. As with the other robots, it marched across the clearing without seeming to notice Bob or Nick.

The robot walked down a narrow, worn path into the woods. Nick knew the colony woods were different from the ones on Earth. The colony trees were thin, smooth cylinders with balls of fluff on top.

The small robot marched through the quiet cluster of trees. It stopped when it came to one tree that looked different from the others. The other trees had smooth, silver trunks that shone in the shadowy light. The strange tree had a gray-green trunk with ragged gouges that leaked a thin, clear liquid. Then Nick saw why.

The robot unfolded a work arm. At the end, a round hole saw spun with a grinding whir. The robot smacked the saw against the tree. It cut into the trunk with a wet sound.

As soon as the cutting began, a low moan rose among the trees. The trunks swayed even though no wind passed through the woods. The saw cut deeper, and the moaning grew louder and louder.

Nick clamped his hands over his ears. "What's making that noise?"

"The only things here are us and them." Bob pointed to the trees. "It is not us. It must be them."

Before Nick could comment, one of the thinnest trees bent down suddenly. It smacked Nick hard with the fluff that topped the stalk. He thought he'd be knocked to the ground. Instead, he stuck to the fluff. The tree hauled him high into the air.

CHAPTER
→» 4 «←

Guess Who Is for Supper

The robot below continued to saw into the wounded tree. More and more trees bent and smacked at the ground. From his spot, Nick couldn't see where the trees struck. He hoped they wouldn't get Bob.

The tree where Nick hung swayed in a wide arc. The sticky fluff held Nick tightly in place. But the rocking made him feel sick. As the swinging finally stopped, so did the moaning in the trees.

Nick found that each small bit of fluff was easy to pull off. But whenever he did, he seemed to find more stuck in other places. The fluff looked so soft and light from the ground. Now it felt like sticky glop. Nick squirmed and picked at the fluff until he could see through the strands to the ground below.

The robot with the saw finished its job. Then it simply turned and stomped away on its four legs. None of the trees touched it. The little robot had no sense of the danger it had been in.

Bob looked up at Nick. None of the trees had touched the tall robot either. Nick sighed in relief. Now Bob could get him free.

"How did the trees miss you?" Nick asked.

"I stood very close to one trunk," Bob said. "The bending trees couldn't reach me without getting stuck to the trunk."

"I wish I'd had time to think of that," Nick grumbled.

"I believe the trees targeted you," Bob said. "These plants have some kind of defense mechanism against attacks by organic life. They are good at finding organic life. They do not seem to be as good at finding robots."

"Lucky you," Nick said.

"Yes," Bob agreed. "Your position looks awkward and potentially dangerous. I am far happier to be where I am."

"I'm glad you're happy."

Suddenly angry, Nick struggled wildly to pull himself free. But he only got more fluff stuck to his clothes. So much fluff covered his arms that he looked like he was turning into a stuffed toy. Finally exhausted, Nick hung almost upside down and panted.

Then Nick thought of the Earth plants in his drawing. He remembered the sundew's sticky fibers that caught bugs. When the sundew caught them, it ate them.

Nick looked down at his hand. Sticky ooze from the fluff touched his skin. It tingled and stung. He yelled down to Bob, "Help! It's going to eat me!"

"What is eating you?"

"The plant. It's like a sundew. All this sticky stuff is going to digest me. Go get help."

Bob shook its head. "I cannot comply with that request."

"What?" Nick shrieked.

"If I notify the colony, I will be blamed for bringing you outside. I will be blamed for using my security codes to open the door. I will be blamed for following the other robot. Your father will be angry. He will turn me off. He will reprogram me or take me apart."

"No, no, it'll be all right," Nick said. "I'll tell them it's all my fault. I promise. Dad won't be mad at you. He'll be glad you went for help. You'll be a hero, Bob."

"You may be right," the robot said.

Nick sighed in relief. "Good. Go get help."

"You may also be wrong. I find the risk to be too high. I cannot inform the adults in the colony."

Bob turned and headed back through the trees toward the colony, leaving Nick screaming for help.

Chapter
→ 5 ←

With the Greatest of Ease

"Help!" Nick screamed as he pulled against the fluff. He hoped a colony scientist would hear him before the tree was done eating him.

As he grew tired, he realized the stinging had stopped. He scraped some fluff off with his fingernails. The skin underneath looked normal. Maybe it wasn't going to eat him. Or maybe it was storing him to eat later. He started struggling again.

Something rumbled below him. Nick wiggled until he could see the ground. Bob clumped along with a small robot trailing at its side.

"I have created a plan for getting you down," Bob said. Nick sighed in relief. Bob tapped the rolling robot and a door opened. A long arm unfolded from inside the robot. At the end, a saw blade began spinning with a worrisome hum.

"Wait a minute," Nick called down. "I don't think it's a good idea to hurt the trees more. That's what started all of this trouble in the first place."

"Trust me," Bob said.

"Maybe we can find a way to calm the trees down," Nick said. "Maybe it would put me down."

"Fungus-based plant life cannot be reasoned with, Nick," Bob said. It tapped the smaller robot again, which made it roll toward the thin tree. It's saw blade began whirling.

"Wait, wait!" Nick yelled. "What happens when you cut down the tree? I don't want to fall to the ground."

"I will catch you," Bob said. "I am 76 percent certain I can do so without breaking any of your primary bones."

"That doesn't make me feel good."

The slow robot finally reached a spot close to the tree. It extended the saw blade toward the smooth, silver trunk. The trees thrashed as if a high wind pushed them back and forth.

"Stop, stop!" Nick yelled. The shaking made his teeth rattle.

Then he realized something. As he was flung around, some of the fluff actually pulled away from his skin. He could move his arms more freely. He could even kick one leg.

"Hey, I'm pulling free," he said. "Keep scaring the tree, but don't cut it."

"I will follow that plan, Nick," Bob shouted up at him.

More and more of the fluff pulled away from Nick's skin and clothes. But the wild ride was making him sick to his stomach. He pulled his arms and legs away from the fluff. He stretched down to grab the smooth trunk. "I think I can get free now," he shouted.

Before Bob could respond, the tree bent toward the ground. Nick let go of the trunk. He hoped to drop the short way to the ground. Too much fluff still hung to his shirt and pants. He only dangled above the ground. "Bob, grab me!" he yelled.

The tree snapped back straight. The quick snap pulled the last of the fluff free. Nick sailed high into the air. He was free! But hitting the ground was going to be very, very bad.

"Bob!" he screamed. But before he could fall, something snagged the back of Nick's shirt. What could possibly grab him that was taller than a tree?

Nick twisted to see. He could hear a buzzing like the saw on the small robot. Then he finally caught sight of what grabbed him. He was looking into the biggest insect eyes he'd ever seen.

CHAPTER
→ 6 ←

Don't Help Me So Much

The creature that held Nick looked a lot like the pictures of Earth bees from his computer tablet. But Earth didn't grow bees this big. Earth grew horses this big. But not bees.

The bee seemed to be having trouble carrying Nick's weight. It was pulled toward the ground as it flew in a wide circle among the trees. Bits of tree fluff smacked at Nick's pants. The movement slowed the bee still more.

Below Nick, Bob ran around with its mechanical arms out. "Try to get free. When you fall, I will catch you!"

"That's a terrible idea," Nick screamed. But he squirmed in the bee's grip. The bee held tight. "It won't let go. Get Dad!"

"No!" Bob yelled back. "I will make it drop you." The robot scooped up a rock with one of its long arms, and threw it hard. The rock missed the bee. It smacked Nick in the seat of his pants.

"Ow!" Nick yelled. "No more rocks!"

Nick figured he better get free before Bob got any more ideas. He remembered how soft the ground felt. He hoped it felt that soft if he fell from so high up.

He squirmed harder as a plan formed in his head. The bee was really only holding onto his clothes. If he could slip out of his shirt, the bee would probably drop him. He wiggled until he heard a ripping sound. Maybe his idea could work. He squirmed harder.

Down below, Bob ignored Nick's command not to throw rocks. A jagged shard of rock barely missed Nick's head. He yelped as the rock sailed by the bee's head too.

The insect's buzzing grew louder, much louder. Clearly, it didn't like the flying rocks.

Nick could see the treetops again. They were flying higher than Nick wanted to fall. They were also flying too fast for Bob to keep up. Nick stopped squirming. The ground was soft. But he didn't think it was *that* soft.

"I will find you, Nick!" Bob shouted.

"Get Dad!" Nick screamed.

Bob shouted something else. The bee had flown too high for Nick to hear it clearly. He suspected the robot had refused again.

Then Nick couldn't see Bob anymore either. They had raced too far away.

The bee's giant, beating wings made a loud buzzing sound. Nick could feel the buzzing in his bones. It made his head ache. It didn't help that hanging below the bee wasn't the least bit comfortable. His shirt nearly choked him, but he didn't dare try to squirm into a more comfortable position.

Below he saw miles of treetop fluff pass by. More and more he wondered if he'd ever see his dad again.

Finally, the bee creature began to fly lower. Nick hoped it was getting tired of hauling him along. Maybe it would land to rest and Nick could get away. But the bee didn't land. It whizzed along very fast. Its buzzing sounded excited somehow. Nick worried that anything that would excite a bee would be bad news for him.

Peering ahead, he saw the fluff trees thinning out. They had come to the end of the fluff tree forest. Below, he didn't see the soft, blue-green moss. Instead, the ground looked black and wet. He wasn't sure he wanted the bee to land in that.

Nick squirmed very gently to see ahead of him. He gasped at the sight. They were flying toward a giant hive. The hive was bigger than the whole colony and much taller. The buzzing of the bee that carried him was echoed by the buzz of dozens of bees flying in and out of the giant hive.

With horror, Nick wondered if this is what happened to his mom and the other explorers. *Did the bees carry them away to this hive? Is that why she never came home?*

He squirmed to see the hive better. Would he find his mom when the bee got to the hive? Or would he just be breakfast for the buzzing creatures?

Before he could find out, he heard another ripping sound from his shirt.

His squirming was too much for it. Nick gave a panicky glance downward. He was still far too high.

Nick held as still as possible. He hoped the last seams held together.

The fabric ripped loudly.

Nick slipped out of the tatters and fell.

CHAPTER
→ 7 ←

In the Deep Dark

Nick plummeted toward the dark ground. For a quick moment, he wished for fluff trees below him. Sure, they might have wanted to eat him. But at least they were soft. That was his last thought before he hit.

To his surprise, the darkness wasn't hard ground. It was black water, or something like it and very cold. He flung his arms around and kicked his legs. He wished he'd learned to swim like Earth kids.

Nick opened his eyes under the black water. No light cut through the darkness. He tried waving his hand in front of his face. All he saw was black.

Under the surface of the black water, something bumped his leg. He wasn't alone in the water. He tried harder to imitate the swimming strokes he saw once in a movie. But was he swimming up or down? Everything was confusing in the dark.

Something bumped him again. And again. Then it stayed under Nick. He felt hard shell under his hands. The creature was moving with him seated on it. But was it going up to the surface? Maybe it just wanted to drown him faster so it could eat him.

Finally, Nick's head popped above the black water. He took a big breath of air. Then he looked down at the shell.

The creature he sat on looked like a bug he had seen in one of his Earth pictures. A shiny, black water bug. Huge round eyes rolled near Nick's hands. Short antennae twitched and turned. Nick jerked his hand back before one could touch his fingers. The bug had long legs that churned like paddles through the water. It also had glistening sharp jaws that snapped together with a loud clack. Was this bug saving his life or just saving him for supper?

The creature raced across the top of the water. The breeze on Nick's wet clothes made him shiver. He hunched down closer to the bug's slick

back. He needed to get off before it dove back underwater. And before they reached wherever it was going. But how? He couldn't jump back into the water. And the creature didn't go close to shore.

Ahead, Nick spotted soggy, pinkish fluff bobbing on top of the black. A fluff tree had fallen over into the water. The trunk was spotted with thick, black slime. The fluff was clumped and discolored. But the tree lay partly in the water and partly on land. Could it be the bridge Nick needed?

The creature headed toward the fallen tree. It was slowly turning aside to avoid smacking into the trunk. Nick didn't want to miss his chance to get to shore.

Slowly, he stood on the back of the beetle. He wobbled and shook, but he stayed on his feet. He remembered pictures he'd seen of people on Earth riding surfboards on the water. Nick wasn't sure if he felt like cheering or puking. Is this how surfers feel? Then when they were as close to the fallen tree as he could hope, he jumped.

For an instant, Nick didn't think he'd jumped far enough. *I really should have spent more time in the gym,* he thought. Then he slammed into the side of the mushy trunk. The bug swam off without him.

Nick hugged the squishy trunk until he stopped shaking. He wrinkled his nose. The tree smelled worse than stinky socks. It smelled worse than the bean cheese his mom loved so much.

Nick was ready to get away from that smell. He began working his way toward the shore. He dug his fingers into the squishy trunk to claw his way along. As he dug his fingers in, goo oozed from the trunk. The green ooze smelled even worse. It stuck to his fingers and his clothes, but he kept going. Hand by hand, he inched his way toward the shore.

His legs still dragged through the dark water. Nick tried not to imagine what might be below. Or how tasty his legs might look. He focused on moving along, one handhold at a time.

Finally, he reached the banks of the black lake. Nick scrambled out. He had never imagined he'd love the feeling of land so much.

Nick was cold and lost. He had no food. He had no drinkable water. He had no idea how to get back to the colony. He looked around. In the distance, he could see the hive, buzzing with workers. Could his mom have ended up there?

On the other side of the lake, he could see the beginning of a forest of fluff trees. That might be the way home. Then he remembered Bob's promise to find him. Was the robot really looking?

He thought about his choices hard. He suspected that choosing wrong might mean never seeing another birthday.

The Ending Is Up2U!

If you believe Nick should head into the hive to look for his mother, turn to page 48.

→ OR ←

If you believe Nick should head back for the colony and hope to meet Bob along the way, turn to page 59.

→ OR ←

If you believe Nick should look for a safe place to wait for Bob to find him, turn to page 70.

ENDING

→ 1 ←

Into the Hive

Nick stood up. He rubbed at the slime clinging to his arms and chest. He wished he had a hot shower and new clothes. But he shook off the idea. Wishing wouldn't fix anything. He had to make a decision right now.

He looked around, wondering where he could wait for Bob. Then he pictured the time he'd spent in the air. Bob couldn't move as fast as the giant bee.

Nick didn't think it was a good idea to wait. He might die of thirst or freeze before the robot ever found him. He needed to do something.

His gaze turned again to the hive. His mom might be inside with the other scientists. His mom was smart. She might have found a way to hide from the bees.

If Nick went to the hive, he had a chance to find his mom. He could help her get home, maybe. He certainly didn't see any other good choices.

He headed in the direction of the giant hive. The ground under his feet had none of the soft moss. Instead it was stained black by the water and strewn with huge rocks.

He could hear fast running water nearby, but he couldn't see it. And, he didn't bother to look. Instead, he kept his gaze on the hive.

The closer he got, the bigger the hive looked. Nick was sure all the colony buildings piled together would still be shorter than the mountain of beehive in front of him. The buzzing was so loud it made Nick's ears and even his bones ache.

Still Nick kept walking.

As he reached the hive wall, he worried he wouldn't be able to find a way into the hive. All the bees were buzzing above his head. He assumed that would be where all the openings into the hive would be as well.

Nick walked around the outside of the hive. He wondered if he would need to climb up the side of the hive to reach the openings overhead.

He pressed his hands to the hive wall. The walls were smooth and warm against his skin when he touched them. The buzzing in the hive made the walls rumble softly. It was creepy but almost pleasant.

The surface had some bulges. But they didn't seem to offer real footholds. Nick wondered if he should try to find something to stick into the wall to help him climb. He decided to keep circling the hive. He could watch for a sharp rock he could use to help him climb.

Nick kept walking, feeling more and more discouraged. He saw plenty of rocks. None were sharp enough to cut into the thick wall.

Then he gave a shout. Up ahead he saw a wide crack in the side of the hive. The crack bulged slightly outward.

Nick peered into the crack. He couldn't see how deep it went. It was too narrow for the giant bees. But it wasn't too narrow for him. At least he hoped it wasn't. He didn't have any other choice.

Nick crammed himself into the crack. He had to shuffle along sideways because it was so tight. Sometimes his chest felt almost squished. He worried constantly that he would get stuck. Or that he'd find the crack didn't go all the way into the hive.

Nick pushed harder into the crack. Finally, it squished him so tightly he couldn't breathe. In a panic, he gave one last hard push. He popped out inside the hive.

He toppled to the floor of the hive. Like the walls, the floor was smooth and warm. He scrambled to his feet. He wondered how often the bees moved through these tunnels. The thought of running into one of the bees made him shiver.

I have to find Mom, he reminded himself.

He picked a direction and started off. He found tunnel after tunnel in the hive. The walls bulged inward in the middle, making a kind of crack along the bottom.

Off and on, he heard one of the bees rustling as it trooped through the tunnels. Nick would drop to the floor and roll into the bottom crack. Each time, the bees didn't seem to notice him as they passed by. Moving through the dark tunnels was making Nick tired. He began to hope for a safe place to stop and rest.

Sometimes he found rooms. He peeked inside, but each time he saw only bees. Bees filling holes in the walls. Bees carrying giant eggs. Bees moving around, buzzing at one another.

He was beginning to think he'd made the wrong choice. His mother wasn't here. And now he didn't know how to get out of the confusing maze of tunnels. All he could do was keep going.

Then he peeked into a room filled with baby bees. Some were pale pink. Some were almost brown. They had stumpy legs and no wings.

Some were only about Nick's size, while others were bigger.

A few grown bees bustled around the babies. The adults crammed bits of food into their mouths. *This must be the bee nursery*, Nick thought.

To Nick's surprise, he spotted a colony scientist in the corner of the nursery. The scientist had grown plump since Nick saw him last. As Nick watched, a bee waddled over. It stuffed a scrap of food into the scientist's mouth. *The bees must think he is a baby!*

Nick quickly scooted across the room. He hid behind baby bees whenever an adult came by. Finally, he reached the scientist. "Doctor," he whispered. "Where's my mom?"

The scientist blinked at him. "What?" He seemed to be half asleep. And he was drooling.

"Come on," Nick said. "We have to get you out of here." He grabbed the scientist's arm and began pulling.

Nick had to get the man to his feet. He pulled and tugged. He even tried smacking the scientist to wake him up. Nothing worked.

Nick felt something sharp poke him in the back. A bee creature stood behind him, holding some food. It started to shove it toward Nick's mouth. Nick ducked down behind the scientist. The food went into the man's drooling mouth.

The bee wandered off. Nick grabbed the back of the scientist's jacket. He slowly dragged him out of the nursery. Just before he reached the hallway, one of the adults spotted him.

It buzzed loudly and marched toward Nick, waving a scrap of food. Nick pulled harder and got the man into the hall. He could see the nursery bee following them. He couldn't outrun a giant bee!

A tiny bee began squeaking near the nursery worker. The adult turned and shoved the food into the baby's mouth. When it wasn't looking, Nick hauled the scientist away. To his relief, the bee didn't follow.

The hallway floor was slicker than the soft nursery floor. Nick was able to drag the man faster on the smooth floor. He stumbled along the dark tunnels, pulling the scientist along with him. Nick knew he should have found the crack already. Somehow he'd gotten lost.

Still, he had no choice. He kept going. The halls grew quiet and dark.

Then, the floor under Nick fell away. Nick sucked in his breath as he and the scientist fell through the darkness. They smacked into racing water. *It must be the water that eventually fed the lake*, Nick thought.

The shock of the chilly water snapped the scientist out of his sleepy daze. Unlike Nick, he could swim. He grabbed Nick and kept him above the water as they raced along.

Soon they were outside in the daylight. The scientist slowly towed them to shore until they were able to scramble out.

As soon as he could talk, Nick gasped out, "Where is my mother?"

The scientist shook his head. "I don't know. We were swarmed by the giant bee creatures. I guess they thought we were lost bee larvae. I didn't see anyone else grabbed. I thought they got away."

Nick slumped. "They didn't make it back to the colony."

The scientist looked up at the sky. "I don't know where your mom is. Or the rest of the team. But I can find our way back to the colony from here. As long as I can see the sun."

"It'll be dark soon," Nick said.

The scientist hauled Nick to his feet. "Then I'll use the stars. You saved me, kid. The least I can do is save you right back."

Nick followed the scientist toward the forest of fluff trees. He looked back at the giant hive. What if his mom were in a different nursery room? Under his breath he whispered, "I'll be back, Mom. I won't give up. I promise."

ENDING
→ 2 ←

A Battle of Giants

Nick slumped to the ground near the black lake. He had to make a choice. The longer he looked at the huge hive, the less he wanted to be inside it. His mom might be in there. But what could he do about that? He wouldn't be much help if a bee ate him.

He needed adults. If he could get back to the colony, he could tell his dad about the hive. Then a team could come and look for his mom. They would know what to do about the giant bees. Maybe Dad would send some of his new robots in to save her.

Nick stood and turned to the hive. He brushed muck from his clothes. "If you're in there, Mom," he shouted, "I'll be back."

Then he turned and started around the outer bank of the lake, toward the fluff forest in the distance. He knew it had to be a long way back to the colony. He turned to look at the hive again. He hoped he was making the right choice.

"I'll hurry," he called back, even though he knew his mom couldn't hear. He trotted across the bare ground. His feet felt heavy. *I have to save Mom*, he thought. He made himself hurry even faster.

By the time he reached the trees, Nick was cold and hungry. He was so tired he could barely pick up his feet. "I wish I had some birthday cake," he grumbled. "Or a birthday cookie." Then he sighed. He'd settle for some birthday lima beans.

He knew part of the reason his mom left was to find local plants they could safely eat. The colony scientists learned they couldn't eat fluff trees. They couldn't eat the moss near the colony buildings either. If they were going to find food, they had to look far from the colony.

Nick looked at a bunch of bushes nearby. The leaves were a pale purple, and round white balls hung from each branch. Nick leaned down to sniff one. It smelled good and made his stomach growl. He wondered if it would be safe to eat.

Nick rubbed his stomach and kept walking. It wouldn't be a good idea to eat any strange plants he found. After all, just being in the same clearing where the little robot poked the fluff trees had already gotten him in enough trouble.

As he imagined different things he'd like to eat, Nick didn't notice the distant clanging sounds at first. But the sounds were getting louder as he walked. Somewhere ahead, someone was banging. Could it be his mom and the scientists? He picked up his pace until he was almost running.

The banging grew louder and louder. Nick slowed up slightly. Did the scientists have anything that could make that much noise?

Maybe rushing toward the noises wasn't his best idea. What if there was something dangerous ahead? Nick slowed until he was barely shuffling forward.

He thought about the surprises he'd found. The fluff trees could move fast. They might whump loudly against the ground. But they were too soft to make the kind of noises he heard. Then there were the bees. But they buzzed and rustled. They didn't clang.

The banging and clanging rang through the woods. They sounded close.

Nick thought of the water bug. The shell was hard. If someone banged on a bug's shell, it might make that sound. His mom and the scientists were smart enough do something like that to signal for help. Maybe it was them after all!

Nick ran through the trees as fast as he dared on the uneven ground. He burst into a large clearing. He saw the clanging did not come from his people at all. He backed up as fast as he could, tripping over a rock and landing on his rear. He stared upward, whimpering softly.

Two giant creatures were fighting. They looked like the ants from Nick's Earth studies program. But ants on Earth had never been so large. These creatures were far bigger than the bees.

The ant creatures clashed and wrestled. Their hard skin made a clanging sound like blades striking armor. Luckily, neither creature spotted Nick.

He scooted the rest of the way to the nearest tree. Though he was scared, he didn't want to go back the way he'd come. He was pretty sure he'd need to get by the ants to find his way home.

Nick looked around the clearing for the best route to avoid the battle. That's when he spotted them. A cluster of five colony scientists stood wedged in the shadow of a huge boulder, half hidden by fluff trees growing close by. Nick squinted, peering at each face. That's when he spotted his mom.

The boulder hid the scientists from the ant creatures. But it also trapped them. Unlike Nick, they couldn't back into the trees without stepping out into the clearing. They were almost under the feet of the battling ants.

Nick couldn't be so close to his mom and not save her. Using the trunk of the fluff tree behind him for support, he slid to his feet. The soft surface of the trunk gave him an idea.

Nick thought about the violent way the trees had reacted when one of them was hurt. He remembered what Bob had said. *Stay close to the tree trunks so they can't grab you.*

Nick reached down and picked up the sharpest rock he could find. He patted the trunk of the tree. "I really am sorry about this." He rammed the sharp edge into the trunk. Then he slammed the rock against the trunk again.

All around the clearing, the trees began to moan and sway. The ants froze. With alarmed chittering sounds, they stopped fighting. They scampered to the center of the clearing, as far from the trees as possible. It wasn't far enough.

The largest of the fluff trees bent double. It swatted one of the ant creatures directly on the back. The tree snapped back up, and the ant went with it. But a giant ant weighed a lot more than Nick. When the tree stopped moving, the ant didn't. It ripped free of the fluff and flew through the air. Nick didn't see it after that.

The other ant panicked. It raced across the clearing to get away. Several trees swatted at it. One even managed to brush the ant's rump. Still each time the trees snapped back, they failed to drag the ant with them.

The giant ant pushed through the trees at the edge of the clearing. The second the ant was gone, Nick raced toward his mom. One of the smaller trees swatted at him. But it missed.

As soon as he reached the boulder, Nick flung himself into his mom's arms. "I found you."

His mom hugged him. Then she held him out at arm's length. "Nick, what are you doing out here?"

"It's a long story," Nick said. "It started with a birthday present."

His mom gave him another hug. "That's right. Happy Birthday, darling."

"I'm having a great birthday now," Nick said. "But why didn't you all come home? Everyone is so worried."

His mom stepped out of the safety of the rock. "I promise to tell you everything. But we need to get going. If this spot is on the regular ant travel routes, we could end up right back in trouble."

Nick opened his mouth to agree. His stomach gave a huge growl. His mom gave him a look, and Nick grinned. "Sorry. I missed lunch. I've had a really busy day."

A scientist wished Nick a happy birthday and gave him an energy bar. Nick had never tasted any birthday treat as good as that bar.

As they walked through the woods, his mom explained that one of their team members was carried off by a giant bee creature.

"I know what that's like," Nick said.

His mom gave him an alarmed look. Then she went on with her story. The team tried to find the missing man, but they lost sight of the bee. They continued on, following the bee's flight direction.

"Of course, that's assuming the bee flew straight." Nick's mom sighed. "We certainly never found him."

"Instead we found the world's biggest ant battle," one of the scientists said.

"I just wish we knew where the bees took him," Mom said.

Nick grinned at her. "I know exactly where the bees took him. I was just there."

His mom stared at him in shock. "It sounds like you really have had quite an adventure."

"You too, Mom. Now, don't you think we better go get your teammate?"

His mom agreed. The rest of the team cheered. With Nick in the lead, they headed for the hive. He snuck a look up at his mom. Nick thought his birthday had turned out okay after all.

ENDING

→ 3 ←

Anything to Survive

Nick stared at the hive for a moment and shuddered. He didn't know if his mom was in there. But he did know the hive was full of scary bees.

He looked back in the direction of the fluff woods. He didn't know if the colony was back that way. He thought it was. But he could just get more and more lost.

He remembered something he'd read once. When Earth kids are lost, they're told to sit down. They had to wait to be found. Anything else would just make you more lost.

Nick didn't need to be more lost. He found a dry rock and scrambled up on it. It gave him a decent view of the area. He laid down on the rock so the sun could dry his clothes. Soon he fell asleep.

He dreamed of scary bees and water bugs with snapping jaws. One of the dream bugs poked him with a long leg. Then it poked him again. "Nick!" the bug said.

That's when Nick woke up to see Bob bent over him. Bob poked his shoulder with one of its long fingers. "You found me," Nick said happily.

"I did," Bob said. "I followed the bee's course through the trees. When I saw the hive, I expected you to be inside."

"I almost was," Nick said. "Instead I ended up in the lake."

The robot looked back toward the dark lake. "I am not designed for interacting with liquids. I am glad you are not in the water now."

"Me too," Nick said.

A long shadow lay over the rock. Nick could see the sun was close to setting. "We better hurry or we'll be walking home in the dark. I don't suppose you have lights? We might need some before we get back."

Bob didn't speak for a moment. The robot continued to loom over Nick. A faint hum came from inside it. "Nick," the robot said finally. "I have very bad news."

"What bad news?"

"When I returned to the colony to get help for you, I found it torn apart."

"Torn apart?" Nick whispered.

"Giant bee creatures. They ripped through the housing and carried off all the people. None of the colony buildings were spared. There is no home."

Nick looked back toward the hive. He could barely see it in the falling darkness. "Then we should go in the hive and look for them. Maybe we can rescue them."

"That is one way," Bob said. "But perhaps we should find your mother and her team. They could help us save the colonists."

Nick put his hands on his hips. "But how are we going to find Mom? And how do we know she's not in the hive already?"

"Coming here, I saw signs of their passage. I believe I can track them."

Nick thought about it for a moment. He looked toward the hulking shadow of the hive. How could one kid save everyone from those giant bees? Bob was right. They needed his mom. And maybe his mom needed them.

"Okay," he said. "Let's go."

For days, they wandered through the woods and over hills. They finally wandered onto a wide plain. It was covered with pale violet stalks of something a little like grass. The stalks held white flowers with sharp petals. They could cut right through Nick's pants. He had to be careful where he walked.

"Are you sure Mom came this way?" Nick asked.

"I am certain," Bob said. "And up ahead I can detect water. We will fill my storage compartment."

Nick knew he was lucky to have Bob. The robot purified all the water they found. And Bob tested new plants to find things Nick could eat. They weren't always tasty things, but at least he wasn't starving.

Still, Nick was getting more and more worried. Would they ever find his mom? Maybe he should have gone to the hive right away. What if he could have saved his dad?

As he shuffled along, Nick could hear the whirr of Bob's insides and the rustle of the grasses in the breeze. Then he realized he was hearing something else. A buzzing sound that grew louder and louder.

"The bees!" Nick yelled.

He took off running with Bob right beside him. The sharp flower petals slashed at his pants. Nick didn't dare slow down. The buzzing grew louder and louder.

Nick looked back over his shoulder. He could see a cluster of bees flying toward them. He ran faster. But they couldn't outrun the flying creatures.

The bees got closer. Nick looked back at them again. What he saw shocked him so much that he stumbled and fell. He rolled through the tall stalks.

Bob didn't stop. The robot kept running.

"Bob, wait," Nick yelled. He pointed back toward the bees.

Now he could see them clearly. On the back of each of the bees sat one of the colony scientists

and his mom. They were riding the bees like horses!

The bees landed, and the scientists hopped off their backs. They patted the bees and walked over to Nick.

His mom turned to one of the other scientists. "Go and get the robot."

When she reached Nick, she held out a hand. "Are you all right? You scared me half to death. We've been looking for you for days."

Nick took her hand. "I don't understand. How come the bees don't carry you away?"

His mom hauled him to his feet and smiled. "We learned how to tame them after we rescued one of our team members. He'd been carried off to a giant hive. Apparently, the creatures thought he was a baby bee." She laughed and the rest of the team joined in.

Nick was still confused. "Did you find Dad at the hive?"

"No, of course not," his mom said. "Your dad doesn't go on expeditions. He's back at the colony. And very worried about you."

Nick turned to Bob as the scientist marched the robot back to them. "Why did you lie to me about the colony?"

Bob bowed its head. "I can't go back to the colony. They'll take me apart." The robot pulled free of the scientist and ran. The scientist pointed a device at it. Bob shook all over before falling to the ground.

"Hey," Nick said. "You didn't have to do that." He ran over to Bob. The robot's soft whirring sounded more like a sick rattle. "Are you all right?"

"I am sorry," Bob said. "I should not have lied to you. I did not want you to go to the colony. I did not want to be all alone."

"I wouldn't have left you alone," Nick said. "Friends don't do that."

Bob rattled louder. "Are we friends?"

"Of course."

"Friends," Bob echoed, then it shut down. The rattling stopped.

Nick turned back to his mom. "You aren't really going to take Bob apart, are you?"

"No, of course not," his mom said. "We just couldn't let it run off. The robot has so much valuable data. But we won't take it apart. We don't destroy something for making a mistake. Besides Bob kept you alive all this time. I guess we owe it one."

Then she pointed at Nick. "But I will tell you this. No more field trips for you two. Not without permission."

"That's fine with me," Nick said. "Let's go home."

And so they did.

WRITE YOUR OWN ENDING

There were three endings to choose from in *Lost in Space*. Did you find the ending you wanted from the story? Or did you want something different to happen? Now it is your turn! Write the ending you would like to see. Be creative!